P9-DCP-075

Jackrabbit Goalie

Weekly Reader Books presents

Jackrabbit Goalie

MATT CHRISTOPHER

Illustrated by Ed Parker

Little, Brown and Company

Boston *Toronto*

This book is a presentation of Weekly Reader Books.
Weekly Reader Books offers book clubs for children from
preschool to young adulthood. All quality hardcover books are selected
by a distinguished Weekly Reader Selection Board.

For further information write to:
Weekly Reader Books
1250 Fairwood Ave.
Columbus, Ohio 43216

Library of Congress Cataloging in Publication Data

Christopher, Matthew F
Jackrabbit goalie.

SUMMARY: Anxious to make friends in a new town, a young boy lies about his experience as goalie in order to get on the local soccer team.
[1. Soccer—Fiction] I. Parker, Edward. II. Title
PZ7.C458Jac [Fic] 78-5438
ISBN 0-316-13975-0

Published simultaneously in Canada
by Little, Brown & Company (Canada) Limited

PRINTED IN THE UNITED STATES OF AMERICA

To Lawrence and Hazel

MIKES

IT WAS just by accident that Pepper heard the kids say that they needed a new goalie.

He stopped walking and turned around.

"A soccer goalie?" His eyebrows raised a notch.

The five kids were standing in front of Mike's Ice Cream Shop. They all looked at him. The tallest one said, "That's right. Who are you?"

"Pepper Pride," said Pepper.

"You're new here, aren't you?"

Pepper nodded. "We just moved here from Columbus, Ohio."

"I'm Bunko," said the tall kid. "This is Johnny, Pat, Gene, and Dick. We play with the Antelopes."

Some of the faces looked familiar. Pepper had seen them here before.

He remembered Mulberry Lane in Columbus. There was a street corner there, too, where the kids stood and talked.

"You mean to tell us you played goalie back in Columbus?" Bunko said, looking Pepper up and down again.

"That's right," said Pepper.

That was a two-foot lie. He played right half, not goalie. But he wanted to make friends. How could he if he didn't exaggerate a bit?

"You're pretty short for a goalie," said Johnny.

Pepper shrugged. "Okay. But if you see me playing goalie on some other team, don't say I didn't tell you."

He started to walk away.

"Hey, wait a minute!" Bunko called.

Pepper stopped and looked at him.

"We have a game at four o'clock," said Bunko. "At Washington Park. If you're so good, we'll see you there."

Pepper flashed a smile. "I'll be there," he promised.

He was there at a quarter to four. The team warmed him up by kicking the soccer ball at him from all directions. He missed a lot of them, got banged and bruised, and wondered if telling a two-foot lie had done him any good.

"I thought you said you were good!" said Bunko.

"I'm out of shape," answered Pepper.

The game started — the Antelopes against the Bears. Bunko passed the ball to Dick. Dick passed it back to Bunko, who booted it down the field toward the Bears' goal.

In another minute Bunko kicked one in for the Antelopes' first goal.

Good, thought Pepper. *Just keep the ball in that part of the field.*

Before he knew it, the Bears were kicking the ball toward *his* end of the field! They were passing it, heading it — doing all those things with it that got it closer and closer to him!

Scared stiff, Pepper waited. The halfbacks tried to stop the stampede, but couldn't. The fullbacks tried to stop it. But they couldn't, either.

Suddenly the ball came flying through the air to Pepper's right side. He dove at it — and made a fantastic catch!

"Nice save, Pep!" Pat yelled.

Again and again the Bears pounded the ball toward the net. But Pepper stopped it every time. Well, almost every time.

"Man, you're a jackrabbit!" cried Bunko. "I wouldn't believe it, if I didn't see it!"

Pepper smiled through the sweat and dirt that smeared his face.

"I — I wouldn't believe it, either," he admitted.

When the game was over he was so tired he wasn't even sure who had won. He asked Bunko.

"We did!" said Bunko. "Four to two! Nice game, Pepper! You were great!"

"Oh, sure," murmured Pepper. He couldn't wait to get home, showered, and in the sack for a long nap.

The Antelopes practiced the next afternoon at the same place. And, for the second day in a row, Pepper got the workout of his life.

Just because of a two-foot lie, he thought.

The more he practiced, the more scratched and tired he got. Out of the whole squad he was the only one who seemed to be really suffering.

He wondered if it was worth it.

Well, yes, it was, he told himself. He had made the team and at least ten new friends. You couldn't make that many friends in five years unless you played on a team. And he had made that many in just one practice.

His heart sang. He felt good — the best since he had moved here from Columbus.

"When is our next game, Bunko?" he asked.

"Next Saturday afternoon," Bunko answered. "And you better be there!"

"Yeah? Why?"

"Because we're playing the Giants! And that's just what they are! Giants!"

Pepper stared at him. "Are they bigger than we are?"

"Most of them are!" Bunko laughed. "But don't let that scare you. We're faster."

"How much faster?"

"We beat them last year by one point," answered Bunko.

"It was a goalie's game," broke in Pat. "You'll have to be on your toes, Pepper!"

Pepper's heart began to pound. Should he confess he really wasn't a goalie?

"See you at the game, Pepper!" said Bunko. "But don't forget the practices, too!"

"I won't," promised Pepper.

He walked home, Pat's and Bunko's words ringing in his ears.

That's just what they are! Giants! It was a goalie's game! You'll have to be on your toes, Pepper!

By the time he arrived home he was sweating almost as much as he had been during practice.

His mother stared at him as he entered the kitchen doorway.

"What war were you in?" she asked him.

"I was practicing soccer," he said. "I'm a goalie."

"A goalie?" His father, a six footer, looked at him. "I thought goalies were tall guys."

"Not all of them," said Pepper's mother, ruffling Pepper's hair. "Look for yourself."

"How come you're playing goalie?" his

father asked curiously. "You played halfback in Columbus, didn't you?"

"They needed a goalie," explained Pepper.

"I see," said his father.

Pepper shrugged. "I had to make friends, Dad. I saw my chance and took it."

"Even if you had to get all scratched up to do it," observed his mother, her eyes sparkling.

He thought and thought about the game against the Giants. He felt that he owed it to the team to play. After all, playing had helped him to find new friends in a very short time.

But, playing against much bigger kids was different. A goalie should not only be fast. He should be tall.

"It was a goalie's game," Pat had said.

Well, this year it won't be a goalie's game with me in there, thought Pepper. *I'm not going to play. That's all there is to it.*

But, how could he get out of it? How big a lie must he think up for this one?

It wasn't till during practice, the day before the game, that he came up with a solution.

He waited till the right moment — and

the right moment came when Johnny booted the ball toward Pepper's left side. Pepper dove at it, and made a great catch.

But he had fallen to the ground — and wasn't getting up.

"Pepper!" cried Bunko. "What's the matter?"

"My ankle!" groaned Pepper. "I think I sprained it!"

"Oh, no!" said Bunko. "Not now! Not the day before we play the Giants!"

The next day, Pepper couldn't sit still at home. And he did not want to go to the game. He just couldn't face his teammates, knowing he was faking an injury.

He decided to go fishing.

He didn't care if he caught a fish or not. It was just something to do.

He did catch one. It was small, about six inches long. *Small, just like me,* he thought, and he tossed it back into the water in disgust.

He kept thinking about the soccer game against the Giants. *You'll have to be on your toes, Pepper! We beat them by one point last year!*

The words kept going through his mind like a haunting song.

Suddenly, he had another strike. He reeled in his line. He had a big one. The fish was giving him a terrific battle.

"Oh, wow!" he cried happily, as he reeled in the biggest fish he had ever caught. It must have weighed at least eight pounds.

Leaving it on the hook, he ran all the way home to show it to his mother and father.

"Mom, Dad — look!" he cried. "Look at the size of this baby!"

"Hey, man! It must have given you quite a fight," said his father.

"It sure did, Dad."

"I thought you had a sprained ankle," his mother said, looking strangely at him. "You ran as if your ankle is perfectly all right."

Pepper blushed.

"It is, Mom," he confessed. "I lied to get out of playing against the Giants."

"Why?"

"Because I thought they might be too big for me. Too strong."

He looked at the fish. "But that fish is big, too. And I pulled it in. I *licked* it!"

He knew then what he was going to do. He took the fish indoors, put it into a pail, and then got into his soccer shorts. "I'll be just in time for the game, Mom and Dad! See you later!"

Bang! The ball sailed toward the inside corner of the Antelopes' net. Pepper dove at it.

A save!

"Beautiful, Pepper!" yelled Bunko.

After a while he made another save. And another.

The big guys, he discovered, were not so big, after all!

He got tired and sweaty, but he played well and felt glad he had come to the game.

2
0
1

Finally, it was over. The Antelopes won, 2–1.

"Pepper, I thought you had a sprained ankle," said Bunko. "You didn't, did you? You just didn't want to face the Giants. What made you change your mind?"

"A fish," answered Pepper, smiling.

Books by Matt Christopher

Sports Stories

THE LUCKY BASEBALL BAT
BASEBALL PALS
BASKETBALL SPARKPLUG
TWO STRIKES ON JOHNNY
LITTLE LEFTY
TOUCHDOWN FOR TOMMY
LONG STRETCH AT FIRST BASE
BREAK FOR THE BASKET
BASEBALL FLYHAWK
SINK IT, RUSTY
CATCHER WITH A GLASS ARM
TOO HOT TO HANDLE
THE COUNTERFEIT TACKLE
LONG SHOT FOR PAUL
THE YEAR MOM WON THE PENNANT
THE BASKET COUNTS
CATCH THAT PASS!
SHORTSTOP FROM TOKYO
LUCKY SEVEN
JOHNNY LONG LEGS
LOOK WHO'S PLAYING FIRST BASE
TOUGH TO TACKLE
THE KID WHO ONLY HIT HOMERS
FACE-OFF
MYSTERY COACH
ICE MAGIC
NO ARM IN LEFT FIELD
JINX GLOVE
FRONT COURT HEX
THE TEAM THAT STOPPED MOVING
GLUE FINGERS
THE PIGEON WITH THE TENNIS ELBOW
THE SUBMARINE PITCH
POWER PLAY
FOOTBALL FUGITIVE
THE DIAMOND CHAMPS
JOHNNY NO HIT
JACKRABBIT GOALIE
SOCCER HALFBACK
THE FOX STEALS HOME

Animal Stories

DESPERATE SEARCH
STRANDED
EARTHQUAKE
DEVIL PONY